For Jackson and Sophia Casbolt

"Excuse me...
is that my
tentacle?"
Alex the Octopus
nervously asks.

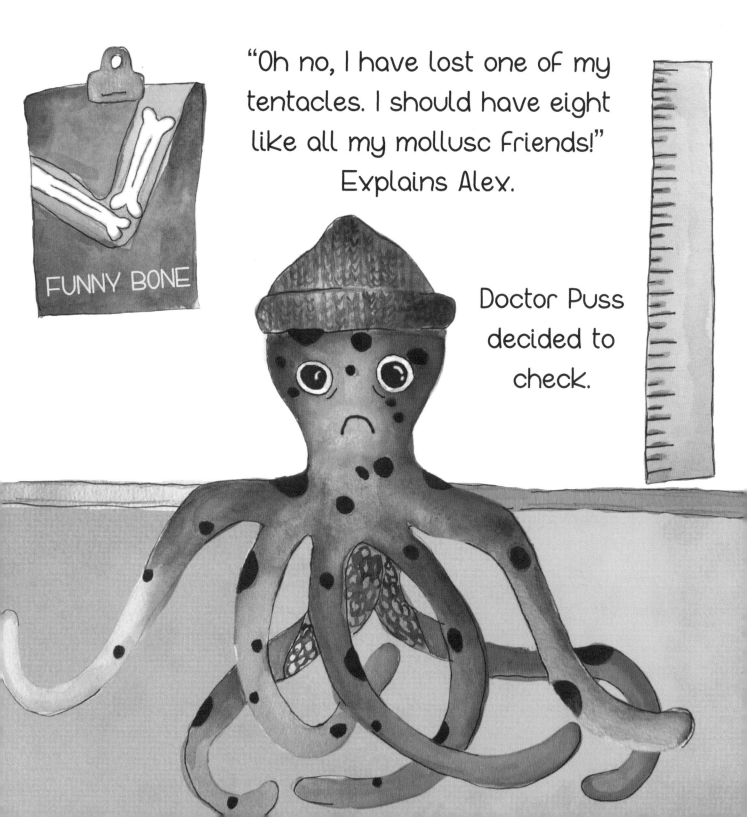

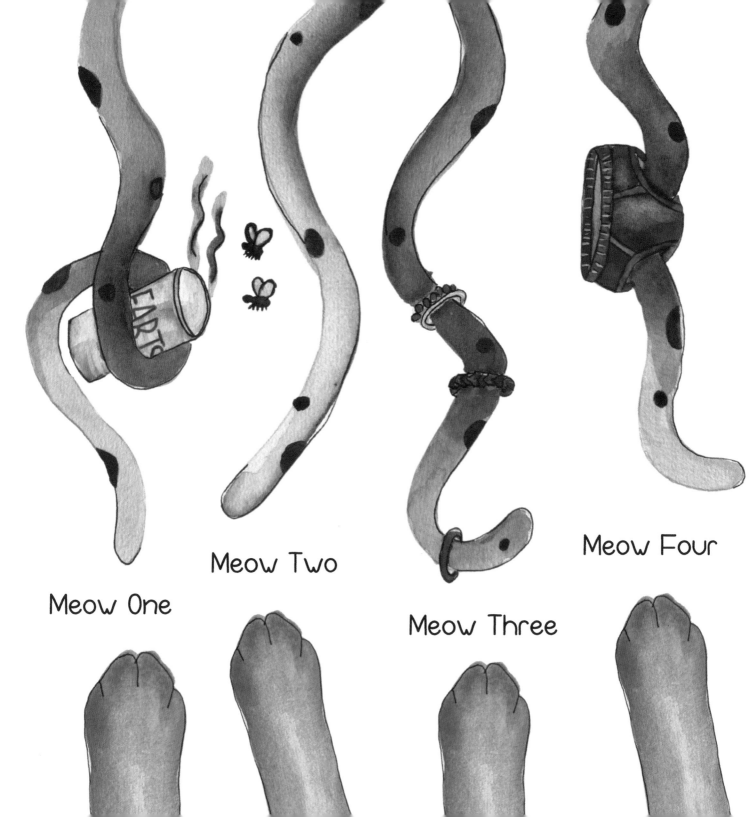

Meow One

Meow Two

Meow Three

Meow Four

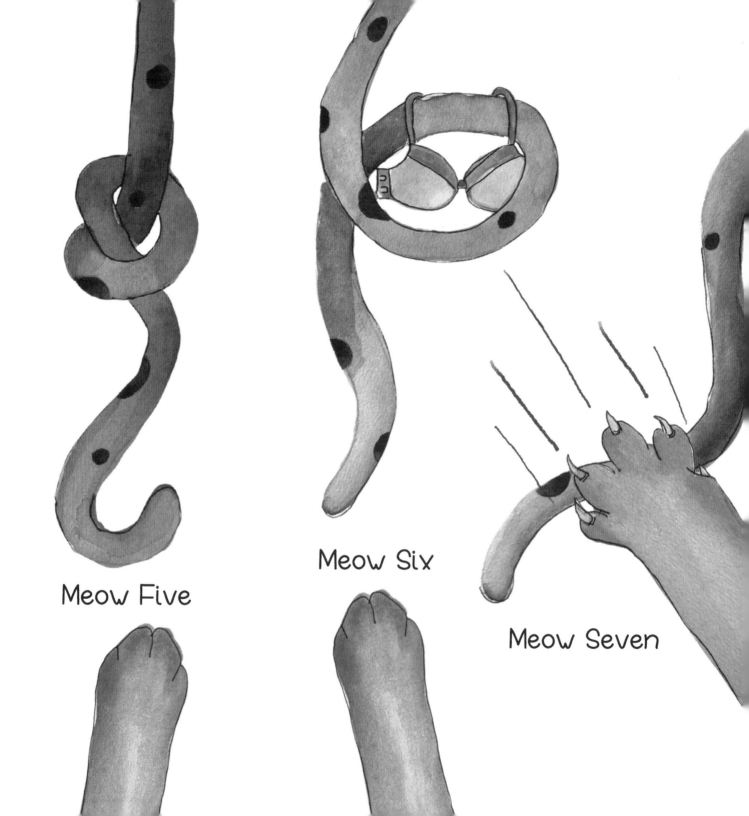

Meow Five

Meow Six

Meow Seven

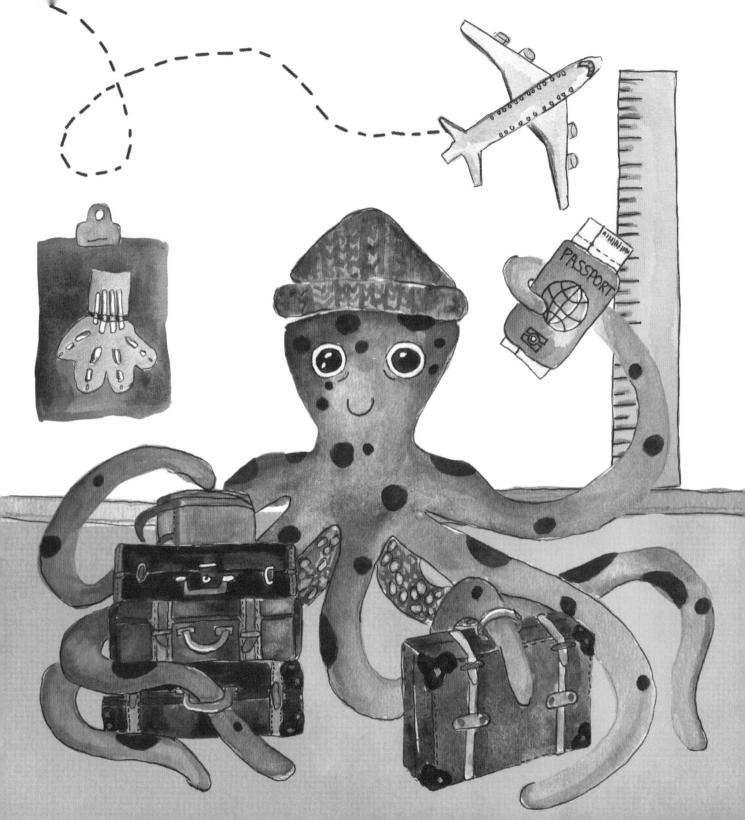

"Yes, here's the one, a trunk of a Borneo pygmy elephant. Curly, long and even comes with a big sucker. It's just purrrrrrrfect!"

The jungle was so humid and sticky, it was no place for an Octopus or a Doctor Puss.

"It's too hot here, this doesn't feel right, it's so wrinkly and chunky."
Alex says sadly.

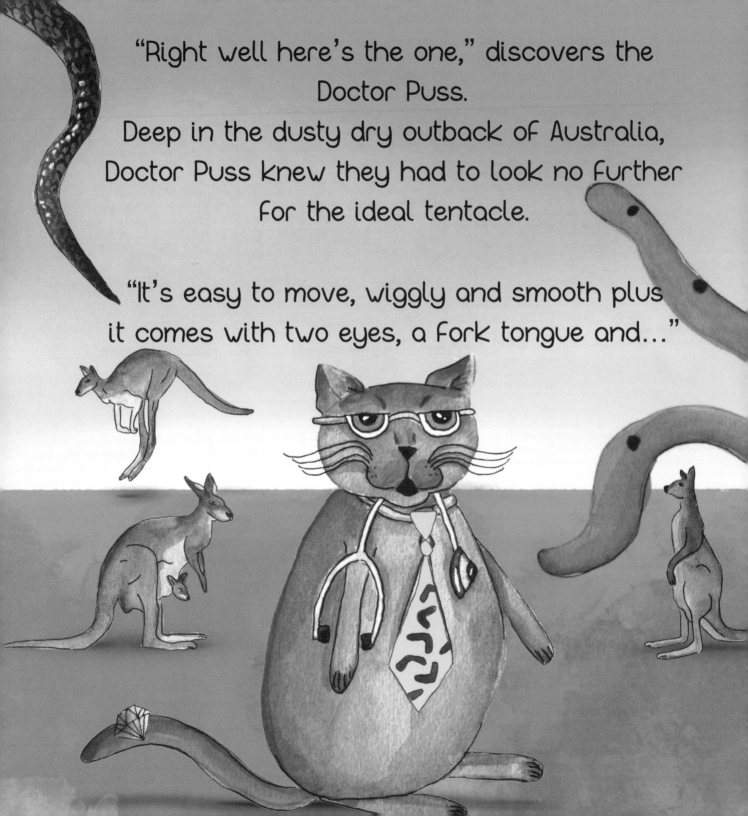

"Right well here's the one," discovers the Doctor Puss.
Deep in the dusty dry outback of Australia, Doctor Puss knew they had to look no further for the ideal tentacle.

"It's easy to move, wiggly and smooth plus it comes with two eyes, a fork tongue and..."

"NO, NO, NO, now that wasn't right," a concerned Doctor Puss mumbled to himself.

"I believe the answer lies far, far away here in New Zealand. A kiwi beak, it might be a bit dark here Alex but the nocturnal kiwi birds are such adorable and charming little creatures. This one will be just splendid!" Explains the Doctor Puss.

"Please no I am scared of the dark," quivers Alex.

"Okay well just try this, a tail of an Egyptian river Nile crocodile, it's scaly, slippery, long and pointy, and precisely what you require."

"It's so enormous, so heavy and way too powerful." Wailed Alex.

The Doctor Puss had nearly exhausted all of his clever ideas. "This is taking up too much of my time, here are some antlers from England. It should be just fine." The yawning Doctor Puss replied.

While the Doctor Puss was snoring away, Alex the octopus decided to try some animals closer to his home in the sea of Santorini.

Alex got thinking…."How about a Flamingo neck? They are curly, curvy and cool."

"Enough! All these animals we have met are unique in their own ways. They are designed perfectly to flourish in their own environments with just what they require.

There is no need to have eight tentacles Alex, you can achieve anything you desire with just seven."

"You are perfect just the way you are."

Can you find a
diamond in the book?

Alexia Stevens has lived in Europe, Australia and Asia. Her home is now in New Zealand with her dreamboat husband and beloved cat Isaac. Her favourite country in the world she has visited is Egypt. Alexia married her soulmate Warren in the stunning island of Santorini, Greece. She has done many things, earnt an interior design degree, travelled the world, worked in retail management, she's a model and now an author and illustrator.

What an adventure she's had.

Even though her life is to be cut short at such a young age,
it has been nothing short of amazing.

Thank you for buying her hand painted watercolour book, you have filled the hearts of many people who love her so much and her constant positive sparkle!

Printed in Great Britain
by Amazon